ᵀᴴᴱ FAMOUS FIVE

SHORT STORIES

FIVE
AND THE
RUNAWAY
DOG

The Famous Five

Timmy   George   Julian   Dick   Anne

HODDER CHILDREN'S BOOKS

First published in Great Britain in 2022 by Hodder & Stoughton

1 3 5 7 9 10 8 6 4 2

The Famous Five®, Enid Blyton® and Enid Blyton's signature
are registered trade marks of Hodder & Stoughton Limited
Written by Sufiya Ahmed. Text © 2022 Hodder & Stoughton Limited
Illustrations by Becka Moor. Illustrations © 2022 Hodder & Stoughton Limited

A CIP catalogue record for this book is available from the British Library.

ISBN 978 1 444 96008 2

Printed and bound in China
The paper and board used in this book are made from wood from responsible sources.

Hodder Children's Books
An imprint of
Hachette Children's Group
Part of Hodder & Stoughton
Carmelite House
50 Victoria Embankment
London EC4Y 0DZ

An Hachette UK Company
www.hachette.co.uk
www.hachettechildrens.co.uk

Enid Blyton

FIVE AND THE RUNAWAY DOG

illustrated by **Becka Moor**

written by **Sufiya Ahmed**

HODDER

Famous Five Colour Short Stories

For a complete list of the full-length
Famous Five adventures, turn to
the last page of this book

CONTENTS

CHAPTER ONE

'I've **never** done anything like this before,' Anne said.

'**Me neither,** but it'll be fun,' said George, giving Timmy a pat.

'And **hard work,**' Julian added.

1

It was the last week of the holidays and Aunt Fanny had asked them to help with a **new community project**. All summer the beach had been **full** of visitors, but **sadly not everyone** had picked up their **rubbish,** and now there were plastic bottles, sweet wrappers and other items **buried** in the sand or drifting in and out with the tide. Lots of locals had volunteered to **clean up the beach** and Aunt Fanny had been collecting rubbish **all week.**

'We told Mother we'd leave after lunch,' George said. 'Has anyone seen Dick?'

'In here.'

Julian, George, Anne and Timmy all followed Dick's voice to the kitchen and **stared open-mouthed** at the sight before them. Dick was wearing **Aunt Fanny's** apron and **beating something** in a big bowl with a wooden spoon. His hair and T-shirt were **covered in flour.**

'As it's Joanna's day off,' he said, **grinning,** 'I thought I'd bake a lemon cake for Aunt Fanny. I wanted to say **thank you** for having us **for the summer.'**

'**That's nice of you,**' Anne said, eyeing some battered lemons on the table. 'Did you squeeze **all** the juice out of these?'

'I **even** added some peel to the mixture,' Dick said proudly, pointing at a golden cake that had clearly just come out of the oven.

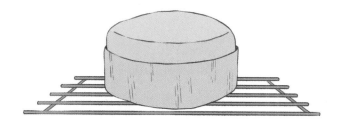

Julian **dipped** his finger in the bowl of icing. 'Did you forget that we agreed to **clean the beach?'**

Dick shook his head and then raised his eyebrows questioningly. 'How does it taste?'

Julian licked his fingertip. **'Tangy.'**

'We need to go!' George said impatiently as she put on her coat.

'Keep your hair on,' Dick said, taking off the apron. 'I'll let the cake cool and then I'll ice it when we get back.'

He wiped the flour from his hair and
T-shirt as they **piled** into the hallway.

'Aunt Fanny left these **rubber
gloves** for us,' Anne said, handing
everyone a pair. 'We have to
wear them to **protect
ourselve**s at the
beach.'

Shortly afterwards the Five were walking down to the beach, enjoying the sun on their faces.

'**Look!**' Dick pointed to a lamppost. '**There's a missing dog.**'

Julian peered closely at the poster that was pinned there.

BELOVED DOG LOST.
NAME: COOKIE.
PLEASE CONTACT MISS BERRY
IF SPOTTED OR FOUND.

'Such a **sweet dog**,' Anne said. 'Look at those **large, floppy ears**.'

'**That's really sad**,' George said. She knew what it was like to love a pet and she felt **very sorry** for the owner. 'I hope the owner and dog are **reunited soon**.'

9

CHAPTER TWO

'**Wow,**' Dick said, looking around at the crowded beach. 'It's a **big turn-out!**'

'**Hello, children!**'

The Five turned to see Aunt Fanny

running towards them, her cheeks flushed.

'Isn't it **wonderful?** So many of the villagers are giving their time. We've had new people **every day** this week. Here are some sacks for rubbish. All this litter in the sea must be **very bad** for the fish and other sea creatures! **Get cracking!**'

They quickly set to work and had managed to fill one of the sacks when Timmy decided it was **time for a game.** He **snatched** the sack from Anne's hand and **ran off** towards the cliffs.

'**Timmy!**' Anne called furiously after him. '**Bad dog!**'

But Timmy loved being chased and dodged all of them. George finally caught up with him and gave him a scolding.

'Not good! Sit.'

Timmy dropped the sack and obeyed with droopy ears. He didn't like it when George told him off.

'**Oh, look!**' Anne exclaimed, holding up a dog collar.

'It looks a bit **water-damaged,**' Julian said, examining it.

'Do you think this might belong to the **missing dog** on that poster?' Anne said, horrified. **'I hope it hasn't drowned!'**

'We can't know,' Julian answered, putting an arm round his sister's shoulder.

'Maybe Timmy can make up for his silly behaviour and help now,' George said. 'Here, Timmy, can you find **the owner?**'

Timmy bounded up, tail wagging, happy to be forgiven. He sniffed the collar, ran towards the sea and then **stopped**. The children watched as Timmy lowered his nose to sniff again before returning to George with a **whimper.**

'He can't pick up the trail,' George said. 'It must have washed away with the tide.'

'Look,' Julian said, noticing something. 'There's a number on the collar. **Let's call it.'**

CHAPTER THREE

Later, the Five left their **full sacks** at the collection point and then walked to the red phone box at the base of the cliffs. They **all piled inside,** including Timmy who got **stuck** between George's and Dick's legs.

'My face is squashed against the glass,' Anne complained.

'I'm getting out,' George announced. **'Good idea!'** Dick and Anne agreed and followed her.

Julian pushed his coin in and dialled the number on the collar. Soon the call was answered. **'Hello, my name is Julian. I found your dog's collar at the beach—'**

'**We** found it!' George protested.

Dick and Anne shushed her.

'**Yes . . . at the beach . . . We were doing a litter pick today . . . Yes, we saw the poster . . .**' Julian reached into his pocket to pull out a little notebook and pencil. '**Yes, go ahead, Miss Berry . . . Right . . . We'll see you shortly.**'

The Five made their way to the village and were soon standing outside a small cottage with a **pink door.** A woman who was about Aunt Fanny's age answered the bell **straight away.**

24

'Hello,' Julian said. 'You must be Miss Berry—'

'You're the boy who called?' she interrupted, looking **frantically** over his shoulder. **'Where is she?'**

'Who?'

'Cookie . . . my dog.'

'Oh, we don't have her,' Anne said.

'But you said . . .' Miss Berry's voice trailed off and her **shoulders slumped.**

'That we found the collar at the beach,' Julian finished.

Sudden tears sprang in Miss Berry's eyes. 'Oh, I thought you'd found my Cookie.'

27

'I'm sorry for the **misunderstanding**,' Julian said. 'Perhaps you could tell us where you last saw Cookie and we'll **try to look for her.**'

Miss Berry wiped away a tear. 'Oh, that is **so kind** of you. I lost her two days ago at the beach. I was so busy collecting rubbish that I didn't notice her **run away. I searched and searched** for her and put up posters all over the village, but no one has seen her.' Miss Berry paused and her eyes grew wide. 'I'm so worried that Cookie might have **run towards the sea and drowned!**'

George stepped forward. 'Let's not think the worst,' she said, almost sounding like Aunt Fanny for once. 'We're going to look for her and **we'll find her.**'

'A photo of Cookie would help us,' Dick added.

Miss Berry nodded. 'I have some extra posters right here. Take one and **thank you** for your kindness.'

Timmy reached up and licked her hand. He **always** knew when a person needed comfort.

CHAPTER FOUR

'Cookie! Cookie!' the four children called as they searched the village square.

'Will your cake be ready for teatime?' Julian suddenly asked.

Dick looked surprised. 'Why do you ask?'

Julian shrugged. 'Because we're going to be **famished.**'

'If we'd headed back to Kirrin Cottage straight after the beach, then yes, it **would** be,' Dick said, checking his watch. **'Now** I'm not so sure.'

'There's a bakery over the road,' Anne said. 'Shall we buy some buns? Aunt Fanny told me about the new owners. Her friends have been telling her how much they **love their cinnamon buns,** which are **absolutely delicious.**'

'Good idea,' Julian said and they both crossed the road.

Something occurred to Anne. 'You don't think Dick's cake will be good, do you?'

'Shh, don't tell him,' Julian said in a low voice.

'**I know you're talking about me,**' Dick said from behind. 'You will **eat your words** after you've **eaten my cake.**'

Timmy began to bark as Julian and Anne entered the bakery.

'**No dogs in here,**' the owner ordered.

'**We're not coming in,**' George called.

'Why is he sniffing the ground like that?' Dick asked.

Julian and Anne emerged with a paper bag of buns and stared at Timmy.

'He's picked up a scent,' George said, and she let go of Timmy's collar. **'Go and find it.'**

Timmy **ran** down the street and turned right into an alley. It was the back entrance to the shops. He **stopped** at a **blue gate** and wagged his tail.

'Woof! Woof!' A bark came from the other side of the gate.

'Oh, you've found a dog,' George said, catching up with Timmy and patting his head. 'Julian, do you think he's found Cookie? He picked up a scent outside the bakery and **led us here.'**

'Maybe,' Julian said. 'Let's see if the dog answers to its name.'

'Cookie!' Dick said loudly.

The dog barked.

'Cookie!' Anne repeated.

George didn't waste another second.

'Hello,' she called, knocking on the gate.

'**Who is it?**' a small voice asked from the other side.

'My name is George, and this is Timmy. We think you have a missing dog.'

The gate creaked open and a young girl with **long black hair** and **wide brown eyes** stared at them. She was clutching a small dog with big, floppy ears. **'How did you find us?'**

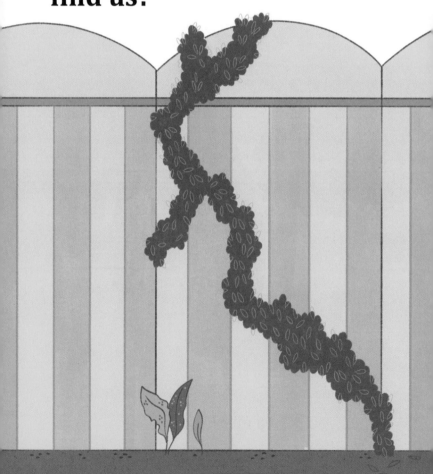

CHAPTER FIVE

'Timmy is **very good** at investigating,' George said proudly as Timmy **wagged his tail.**

'What's your name?' Julian asked.

'Simi. Are you here to take **Treacle?'** she asked nervously.

'Who's Treacle?' Dick asked.

Simi looked down at the dog.

'Ah,' Dick said. 'Where did you find Treacle?'

'Two days ago in Tidy's Garden. She looked frightened and lost. She was hiding under some bushes, so I brought her here.'

'**Why didn't your parents try to find her real home?**' asked George **sharply**.
She didn't approve of dogs being **taken from their owners.**

'Because they don't know,' Simi admitted **sheepishly.**

'Your parents don't know that you have a dog!'

Anne exclaimed.

Simi nodded. 'I hid her in the shed where I've made a little **bed with cushions,** and I gave her **water** and some **biscuits** every day. We moved here a few weeks ago and I don't have any **friends.** Mummy and Daddy are busy with the bakery. They have to make sure all the cakes and buns are **freshly made and sold**.
But Treacle is my friend!
I don't feel so **lonely** when I'm with her.'

George suddenly felt very sorry for the girl. It must be awful not to have friends.

'Do you go to Tidy's Garden to play?' Julian asked kindly.

Simi buried her face in the dog's fur. 'I do, but I don't know any of the other children and they never ask me to play.'

'Well, why don't you meet us at Tidy's
Garden **tomorrow after lunch** and we'll talk
to the other children?' Julian said. 'I'm sure
they'd **love** to include you in their games once
they realise you want to join in.'

Simi looked at him and smiled.

'But we need to **return** Cookie to her owner today. She's missing her dog **very much**,' Julian said.

'**Cookie?**' Simi repeated.

'**Woof!**' the dog barked in answer to her name.

Simi clutched the dog tighter. 'I know I have to give Treac— I mean Cookie back, but I'm really, really going to miss her. Can I come along?'

The four older children **nodded** and Simi smiled.

'I just need to tell Mummy that I'm going out,' she said. **'Wait for me!'**

CHAPTER SIX

Soon the Five, Simi and Cookie were on their
way to Miss Berry's house.

Cookie **barked excitedly** as they
approached the cottage.

The door **flung open** and Miss Berry ran out. Cookie **jumped down** from Simi's arms and into her owner's.

'Cookie! Oh, I missed you!' Miss Berry cried as the dog licked her face.

'I think Cookie's glad
to be home,' Simi
said quietly.

Miss Berry turned to them. **'Thank you SO much for finding her.** Come in. Come in.' She led them inside and offered them **glasses of lemonade.** 'Where did you find her?'

'This is Simi,' Julian said. 'She found Cookie in Tidy's Garden. We think Cookie must have run up to the clifftop from the beach.'

'She was hiding under some bushes,' Simi explained. 'She looked **very scared.**'

'Oh, my poor baby,' Miss Berry said, cuddling Cookie close. 'I've been looking for her **everywhere.**'

'We had fun together and I wanted to keep her for a bit longer,' Simi admitted, looking down. 'I know it was wrong and **I'm sorry.**'

Timmy turned around to lick Simi's hand. He liked the little girl and didn't want her to be sad.

Miss Berry gazed at Simi's bent head. 'Well, Cookie's back home now. I was just very worried that she would get hurt.'

'Oh, no!' Simi's head shot up. **'I made her a bed and gave her food and water.'**

'I'm very pleased with the way you looked after her, and I would like to give you a **reward,**' Miss Berry said. 'What would you like?'

'My own dog,' Simi said sadly.

'Would your parents let you have one?'

'Yes, my daddy said I can, but he's been too busy to get me one. He and Mummy work very hard.'

'Well, I bet you didn't know that Cookie will be having some puppies very soon,' Miss Berry said, patting Cookie's tummy gently. 'Would you like one?'

Simi's eyes grew wide with wonder. **'Could I really? My own dog?'**

Miss Berry smiled and nodded.

Simi beamed. **'Yes, please!** I would love that. I'll look after it and keep it safe and it would be my **best friend.'**

'You may have one of Cookie's puppies if your parents agree,' Miss Berry said. 'Until then you can come and play in my garden with her any time you like.'

CHAPTER SEVEN

The Five dropped Simi back at the **blue gate.**

'We'll see you at Tidy's Garden
tomorrow,' Anne said. 'Be ready to make lots of
new friends.'

'I'm a little bit **scared,**' Simi said, looking nervous.

'Don't worry!' George said. 'You can tell them **all** about Cookie and soon you'll have your very own beautiful new dog. You won't feel **shy** with a puppy by your side!'

'I can't wait,' Simi said, smiling widely. 'See you tomorrow.'

At Kirrin Cottage Dick stepped back to admire his cake. He had just finished icing it and was ready to present it to the others. **'Who wants cake?'** he called.

Julian, Anne, George and Timmy trooped into the kitchen.

'Should we **wait** for Aunt Fanny to come home before we cut it?' Anne asked.

'I say we taste it first,' George said.
'I'm famished.'

Dick cut a slice and divided it into four portions. Anne took the first bite. Her face fell as she **chewed slowly**. Dick didn't notice as he handed Julian and George their share. They **popped** it into their mouths and then **swallowed hurriedly**.

Dick's wide smile disappeared as soon as he took a big bite for himself. The cake was awful. He must have squeezed too much lemon in because it tasted like bitter medicine.

'Woof!' Timmy impatiently barked, grabbing one end of the tablecloth. He wanted his share of the cake.

'Timmy, watch it,' George warned. **'Don't—'**

But it was **too late.** Timmy pulled the cloth and the cake **toppled** on to **his head.**

There was a moment's silence as the children stared at poor Timmy's **cake-covered head.** Then George **burst into laughter** and the others joined in. Timmy wagged his tail happily and gobbled up as much of the cake off the floor as he could.

'I'm sorry we won't be able to eat the rest of the cake, Dick,' Julian said.

'Yes, bad luck,' Anne chimed in.

'Mother will be so sad not to have had a slice,' George said kindly.

Dick knew they were secretly happy not to have to eat any more. To tell the truth, so was he. He shrugged. **'It's OK.'**

'Come on, everyone,' Anne said, **grabbing a cloth.** 'We'd better get this place clean before Aunt Fanny returns.'

71

In no time the kitchen was **spotless,** and they'd just sat down for tea when Aunt Fanny walked in.

'Did you have a nice day?' she asked, collapsing into a chair.

'We did,' Dick answered. 'Here, Aunt Fanny, have a **cup of tea** and one of these new buns we bought especially for you. We'll tell you all about our **adventure** today, starting with a **runaway dog . . .'**

If you enjoyed this Famous Five short story, there's plenty more action and adventure in the full-length Famous Five novels. Here is a list of all the titles, in the order they were first published.